D0603002

For Andrew and Margaret Judge, with thanks S.G.

For Mum and Tim T.T.

First published in the United States 2002 by
Phyllis Fogelman Books
An imprint of Penguin Putnam Books for Young Readers
345 Hudson Street
New York, New York 10014
Published in Great Britain 2001 by
Gullane Children's Books
Text copyright © 2001 by Sally Grindley
Illustrations copyright © 2001 by Thomas Taylor
All rights reserved
Printed in Belgium
1 3 5 7 9 10 8 6 4 2

Library of Congress Cataloging-in-Publication Data
Grindley, Sally.
The sorcerer's apprentice/retold by Sally Grindley; illustrated by Thomas Taylor.
p.   cm.
Summary: A sorcerer's young apprentice attempts to practice magic
in his master's absence, with disastrous results.
ISBN 0-8037-2726-7
[1. Fairy tales. 2. Magic—Fiction.] 1. Taylor, Thomas, date, ill. II. Title.
PZ8.G885 So 2002
[E]—dc21   2001028144

The artwork for this book was created using inks and
colored pencils on watercolor paper.

The Sorcerer's Apprentice

Retold by Sally Grindley

Illustrated by Thomas Taylor

Phyllis Fogelman Books New York

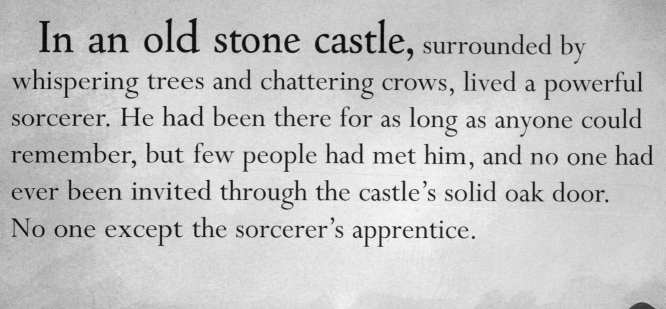

In an old stone castle, surrounded by whispering trees and chattering crows, lived a powerful sorcerer. He had been there for as long as anyone could remember, but few people had met him, and no one had ever been invited through the castle's solid oak door. No one except the sorcerer's apprentice.

The apprentice had been
chosen by the sorcerer
to help him.

"Work hard, my friend,"
the sorcerer had said to him,
"and in time I will teach you
everything I know."

The apprentice couldn't
wait to follow in his
master's magic steps,
and was happy to do
everything he was asked.

He spent hours in the woods digging up worms and catching rare beetles. He collected tree bark and plant roots until his hands were sore and his back aching.

Back in the castle kitchen he crushed and ground them into powder.

And when he had finished, he rushed up and down stairs tidying and cleaning up after his master.

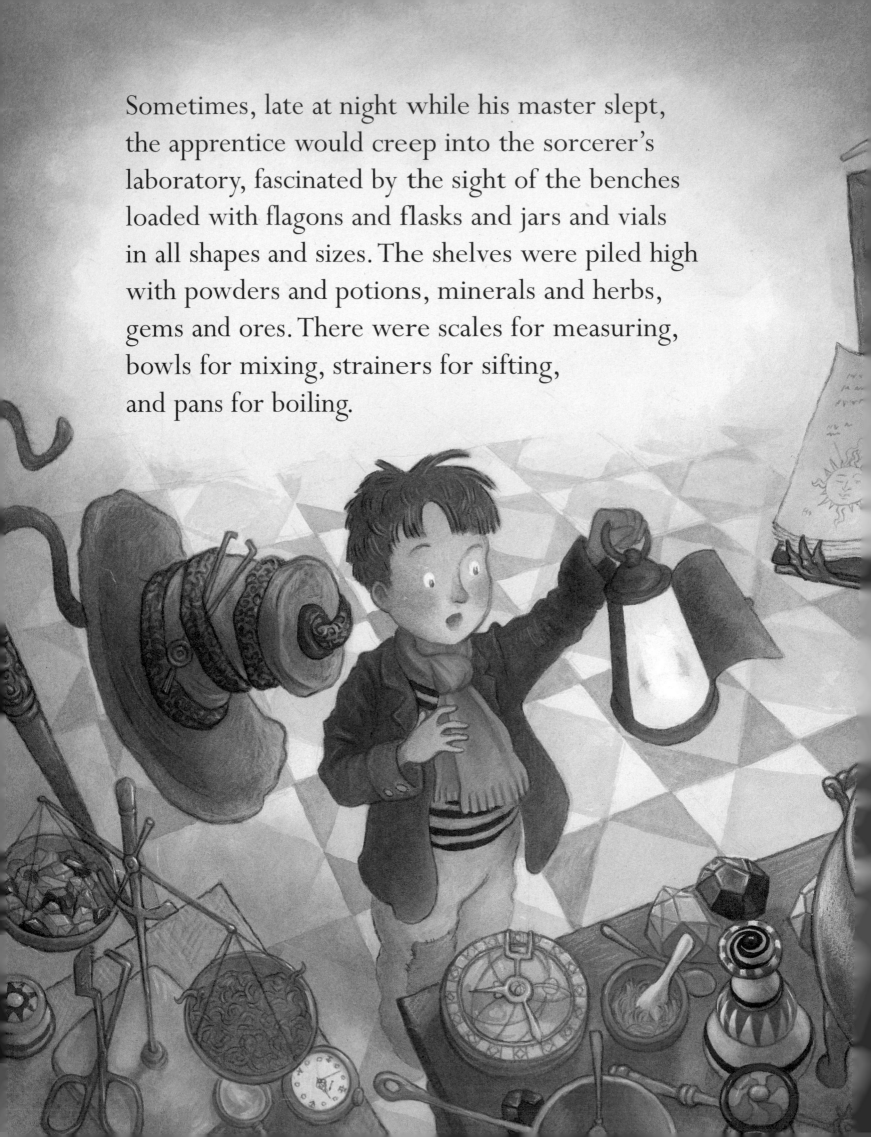

Sometimes, late at night while his master slept, the apprentice would creep into the sorcerer's laboratory, fascinated by the sight of the benches loaded with flagons and flasks and jars and vials in all shapes and sizes. The shelves were piled high with powders and potions, minerals and herbs, gems and ores. There were scales for measuring, bowls for mixing, strainers for sifting, and pans for boiling.

The apprentice would wave his arms around and mutter magical-sounding words, pretending to cast spells, while mixing drops of liquid the sorcerer had left for him to put away. He longed for the time when he could make real magic.

"One day I'm going to be a great magician," he told the sorcerer's cat. "Just you wait and see."

But every time the apprentice asked to be allowed to try a spell, the sorcerer would reply, "Patience, my friend. It has taken me a whole lifetime to learn the secrets of my science. Your time will come."

The apprentice tried to be patient, but as the months passed by, he grew more and more unhappy.

"I'll be an old man before he lets me do any spells," he grumbled to the sorcerer's cat.

Then, one morning, the sorcerer called the apprentice to him.

"I am going across the hills to visit a great sorcerer friend," he said. "I shall need plenty of hot water when I return at dusk. Please fill our largest cauldron and have it ready for me."

The apprentice sat down miserably.
"It will take me a hundred trips to
the well to fill up the cauldron."
Then he had an idea.

As soon as the sorcerer left, the apprentice crept into the great hall and pulled out one of the ancient spell books he had seen his master reading. He pulled out another, and flicked through them all until, at last, he stopped and shrieked with excitement. "This is it!" he cried. "I'll show my master that I'm ready!"

The apprentice raced back to the kitchen and picked up an old broomstick.

"Watch this!" he called to the sorcerer's cat.

He grasped the broomstick tightly with both hands, took a deep breath, and said . . .

"Broomstick, listen to my spell,
Fetch me water from the well.
Fill the cauldron to the top,
Keep on going till I tell you Stop!"

Then he closed his eyes and carefully
chanted seven magic words . . .

The broomstick leapt from his hands. The apprentice watched in amazement as it grew arms and legs.

He stared with wonder as it flung open the castle's huge oak doors and marched off down the path to the well.

He gasped with astonishment as it filled two buckets with water, marched back up the path, through the doors, down the steps, and into the castle kitchen. It emptied the buckets into the cauldron and set off again for the well.

The apprentice clapped his hands with glee.

"I've done it!" he cried to the sorcerer's cat. "I can make magic."

The sorcerer's cat fled from the castle.

The apprentice sat down to watch the broomstick at work. Back it came with more water, then off again to the well. Back and forth. Back and forth.

He started to think of all the other spells he would try. Soon he was carried away with dreams of turning pebbles into sticky toffees, making the sun shine in the night, paddling in rivers of gold . . .

The apprentice woke with a start. *Paddling?* He looked down. The kitchen floor was covered with water. The broomstick was just emptying two more buckets into the cauldron, which was already overflowing.

"Stop! Stop!"

shrieked the apprentice.

The broomstick marched on across the floor.

"Stop when I tell you!" cried the apprentice again.

But the broomstick climbed the steps and went out through the huge doors.

The apprentice found to his horror that he couldn't remember the magic words that would break the spell. He ran down the path shouting after the broomstick. But nothing would stop it.

In desperation, the apprentice grabbed the axe that he used for cutting firewood. As the broomstick emptied the buckets, he chopped it into dozens of pieces.

But no sooner had the pieces fallen, than they too grew arms and legs, leapt to their feet, and marched off to the well. Then back they came, a whole army of them. They shoved past the apprentice and marched relentlessly onwards, determined to carry out his command.

The waters rose up and up. The apprentice cried out with terror. He lost his footing and fell—splash!—into the water.

"Help!" he cried. "Help me!"

And help came.

A powerful voice bellowed
seven magic words.

Everything became still and the water seemed
simply to drain away and just disappear.
The extra pieces of the broomstick joined into
one, and it stomped off to the corner of the kitchen

The apprentice stood in the middle
of the room, dripping wet and shivering.
"I trusted you," said the sorcerer quietly.
"I'm sorry, sir," whispered the apprentice.
"I have let you down."

"You have been very foolish to meddle with things you don't understand," said the sorcerer. "Only the wise may share the secrets of the universe. I should send you away."

"Just one chance is all I ask," pleaded the apprentice. "I know I will be a good magician, I know it."

The sorcerer looked at his apprentice and saw
the eagerness in his eyes.

"Perhaps I have held you back for too long," he
said. "I will give you one chance, but be sure you
reach out and grab it with both hands."

"I will, I promise!" cried the apprentice.
"Then come with me," replied the sorcerer,
"and we will make a start."